For the lovely, one and only,
Bestest-ever Mummy, Joni!
– *P.M.*

For my little ones, Matthew and Beth
– *L.B.*

First published 2012 by Macmillan Children's Books
a division of Macmillan Publishers Limited
20 New Wharf Road, London N1 9RR
Basingstoke and Oxford
Associated companies throughout the world
www.panmacmillan.com

ISBN: 978-0-230-75929-9 (HB)
ISBN: 978-0-330-54570-9 (PB)

1 3 5 7 9 8 6 4 2

A CIP catalogue record for this book is available from the British Library.

Printed in China

# My Mummy

Written by
Paula Metcalf

Illustrated by
Lucy Barnard

**MACMILLAN CHILDREN'S BOOKS**

I could travel round the world
And know I'd never find

A mummy even half as nice
Or brilliant as mine!

She wakes up singing happy songs,
Just like the morning birds . . .

But doesn't always know the tune,

Or many of the words!

Mum and I love cycle rides,
We're speedy as can be

Racing down the hilly bits,

Ready · · ·

steady · · ·

wheeeeeeeeeeeeeeee!

And if I fall and hurt my knee,
She magically appears

To pick me up and hold me tight,

And wipe away my tears.

Mummy's meals are always fun,
She boils and bakes and roasts,
And loves inventing recipes
Like mashed up peas on toast!

Every day we go to feed
The ducklings by the lake –
It turns out that they really love
The dinners Mummy makes!

When it comes to playing games,
No one can compare,

She gives me bouncy horsey rides

And swings me in the air!

She helps me make
fantastic things

paint,

With tin foil,

and string,

Like supersonic rocket ships
With shiny, silver wings!

But if those rockets don't take off

Or head for outer space,

My mummy knows just how to put
The smile back on my face!

She washes me from top to tail
When the day is through,

And after all the splashy fun,
My mummy's cleaner too!

Then she tucks me into bed
While singing lullabies.
We read my favourite storybooks
Until I close my eyes.

When I'm with my mummy
I'm happy as can be,
I thank the moon and stars above
That she belongs to me!